My dear Rose,

On the Planet of Music, I met two kindred spirits who loved each other despite their differences. I realized that there's no limit to what love can accomplish. Every day I'm learning a little more about the grown-up world—and about myself.

How would I react if you or Fox were in danger? Would I be able to think clearly, or would my feelings force me down the Snake's path? I hope I never have to choose between you or Fox and what's best for the universe—but the Snake keeps trying to find a way to make me choose. Why? What's his goal?

I'll try to learn more now that we're approaching a new planet, this time with a lush forest.

Is the Snake really there?

The Little Prince

First American edition published in 2012 by Graphic Universe™.

Le Petit Prince™

based on the masterpiece by Antoine de Saint-Exupéry

© 2012 LPPM
An animated series based on the novel *Le Petit Prince* by Antoine de Saint-Exupéry
Developed for television by Matthieu Delaporte, Alexandre de la Patellière, and Bertrand Gatignol
Directed by Pierre-Alain Chartier

© 2012 ÉDITIONS GLÉNAT
Copyright © 2012 by Lerner Publishing Group, Inc., for the current edition

Graphic Universe™ is a trademark of Lerner Publishing Group, Inc.

Graphic Universe™
A division of Lerner Publishing Group, Inc.
241 First Avenue North
Minneapolis, MN 55401 U.S.A.

Website address: www.lernerbooks.com

Library of Congress Cataloging-in-Publication Data

Dorison, Guillaume.
    [Planète de Jade. English]
    The planet of Jade / by Maud Loisillier and Diane Morel ; adapted by Guillaume Dorison ; based on the masterpiece by Antoine de Saint-Exupéry ; illustrated by Élyum Studio ; translation: Anne Collins Smith and Owen Smith. — 1st American ed.
        p.   cm. — (The little prince ; #04)
    ISBN: 978-0-7613-8754-1 (lib. bdg. : alk. paper) 1. Graphic novels. I. Loisillier, Maud. II. Morel, Diane. III. Smith, Anne Collins. IV. Smith, Owen. V. Saint-Exupéry, Antoine de, 1900-1944. Petit prince. VI. Élyum Studio. VII. Petit Prince (Television program) VIII. Title.
    PZ7.7.D67Pgj 2012
    741.5'944—dc23   2011051719

Manufactured in the United States of America
1 — DP — 7/15/12

THE NEW ADVENTURES
BASED ON THE MASTERPIECE BY ANTOINE DE SAINT-EXUPÉRY

The Little Prince

THE PLANET OF JADE

Based on the animated series and an original story by Maud Loisillier and Diane Morel

Design: Élyum Studio
Adaptation: Guillaume Dorison
Artistic Direction: Didier Poli
Art: Zedarkcrystal
Backgrounds: Isa Python
Coloring: Karine Lambin
Editing: Marco Allard
Editorial Consultant: Didier Convard

Translation: Anne and Owen Smith

Graphic Universe™ • Minneapolis • New York

★ THE LITTLE PRINCE

The Little Prince has extraordinary gifts. His sense of wonder allows him to discover what no one else can see. The Little Prince can communicate with all the beings in the universe, even the animals and plants. His powers grow over the course of his adventures.

The Prince's uniform:
When he wears the uniform of a prince, he is more agile and quick. When faced with difficult situations, the Little Prince also carries a sword that lets him sketch and bring to life anything from his imagination.

His sketchbook:
When he is not in his Prince's clothing, the Little Prince carries a sketchbook. When he blows on the pages, they take wing and form objects that he'll find very useful. Like his sword, it's powered by stardust collected on his travels.

★ FOX

A grouch, a trickster, and, so he says, interested only in his next meal, Fox is in reality the Little Prince's best friend. As such, he is always there to give him help, but also just as much to help him to grow and to learn about the world.

★ THE SNAKE

Even though the Little Prince still does not know exactly why, there can be no doubt that the Snake has set his mind to plunging the entire universe into darkness! And to accomplish his goal, this malicious being is ready to use any form of deception. However, the Snake never takes action himself. He prefers to bring out the wickedness in those beings he has chosen to bite, tempting them to put their own worlds in danger.

★ THE GLOOMIES

When people who have been "bitten" by the Snake have completely destroyed their own planets, they become Gloomies, slaves to their Snake master. The Gloomies act as a group and carry out the Snake's most vile orders so as to get the better of the Little Prince!

7

MICA?

SWEETHEART, LET ME INTRODUCE THE LITTLE PRINCE AND HIS FRIEND FOX.

I RESCUED THEM FROM THE BRAMBLES.

HELLO, LITTLE PRINCE AND HIS FOUR-FOOTED FRIEND.

THIS IS MY GIRLFRIEND...MY LITTLE DIAMOND... ONYX.

INCREDIBLE! YOU'RE SOFT, JUST LIKE CLAY...

YES, YES... STOP, THAT TICKLES!

GREAT, YOU'RE ALREADY MAKING NEW FRIENDS.

DON'T WE HAVE A SNAKE TO CATCH?

HA HA...YES, I'M SORRY. FOX IS RIGHT.

WHAT'S GOING ON HERE? ARE THE BRAMBLES CONNECTED TO MICA'S DISAPPEARANCE?

MY BROTHER MICA BUILT THIS CITY, LAZULIS, TO PROTECT US FROM THE ENDLESS ATTACKS OF THE BRAMBLES.

BUT HE REALIZED THAT OUR RAMPARTS WOULDN'T HOLD FOREVER.

THE BRAMBLES ARE GETTING MORE AND MORE AGGRESSIVE, SO MY BROTHER LEFT TO LOOK FOR THE MAGICAL STONE SEEDS. ACCORDING TO LEGEND, THEY WOULD ENABLE US TO BUILD GIGANTIC WALLS. BUT WE'VE HAD NO NEWS OF HIM.

I SEE. BUT WHY HAVE THE BRAMBLES SUDDENLY BECOME SO VIOLENT? COULDN'T THE SNAKE BE BEHIND ALL THIS?

WHAT'S HAPPENING?

IS IT DINNERTIME?

IT'S THE ALARM. THE BRAMBLES ARE ATTACKING!

HELP!

19

OF COURSE! I WANT MY PEOPLE TO BE HAPPY. IF A HERO LIKE YOU CAN BRING BACK MY SON SO WE CAN STAY HERE, I WOULD BE DELIGHTED.

BUT THAT'S IMPOSSIBLE! THE JUNGLE IS HUGE, AND ONLY MICA KNEW WHERE TO LOOK FOR THE STONE SEEDS...

...WITHOUT MY FLYING ARCH, WE COULD SPEND YEARS LOOKING AND NEVER FIND HIM!

WE DON'T HAVE ANY CHOICE. WE HAVE TO TRY, WHATEVER THE COST.

WE'LL LEAVE AS QUICKLY AS POSSIBLE. JADE, YOUR SON WILL BE HOME SOON.

THANK YOU, LITTLE PRINCE. I KNOW YOU WON'T DISAPPOINT US.

DON'T WORRY. I KNOW WHAT WE'RE FACING.

WERE YOU LISTENING TO WHAT YOU JUST SAID?

DON'T YOU UNDERSTAND? JADE IS PROBABLY IN LEAGUE WITH THE SNAKE.

NO ONE EVER RETURNS FROM THAT FOREST, AND SHE'S HOPING WE'LL JUST DISAPPEAR.

25

35

WHERE DID THE LITHIANS GO?

ONYX HAS ALREADY LED THEM TO THE ARCH. THEY'RE WAITING FOR US TO GET THERE WITH THE CRYSTAL.

PERFECT.

HURRY, WE MUST ACTIVATE THE CRYSTAL!

THE END

The Little Prince

AS IMAGINED BY
MATTHIEU
BONHOMME

53

Antoine de Saint-Exupéry
Aviator • Author • Adventurer • Hero

Antoine de Saint-Exupéry, author of the novel *The Little Prince* on which these new adventures are based, was born on June 29, 1900, in Lyon, France. He was the third of five children: Marie-Madeleine, Simone, Antoine, François, and Gabrielle. It was when he was twelve years old, during his summer break from boarding school, that airplanes and flying first made a huge impression on him.

In 1920, he was accepted into the École des Beaux-Arts in Paris to study architecture, but the next year he joined the Second Aviation Regiment of the armed forces and received his pilot's license. In 1922, he had his first plane crash and suffered a head fracture. He had to leave the armed forces and work at different jobs on the ground to earn a living.

By May of 1926, Saint-Exupéry was able to fly again. He delivered airmail, which was a new and sometimes dangerous profession, on routes from France to Senegal and all the way to South America. That was where, in 1931, he met and married Consuelo Suncin.

From 1933 to 1938, Saint-Exupéry was very busy. He traveled to North Africa and Indochina and attempted to break the flight speed record from Paris to Saigon, Vietnam—during which his plane crashed again. It went down in the middle of the Sahara Desert. After his recovery, his life became even busier. He wrote newspaper reports in Spain on the Spanish Civil War, scouted airplane routes between Casablanca and Timbuktu, wrote a screenplay, registered several patents, and traveled to the United States. In 1939, with the start of World War II, he returned to France and talked his way into a job as a high-risk reconnaissance pilot for the French Air Force. But this only lasted until France reached an armistice agreement with Germany.

In December 1940, Saint-Exupéry returned to visit friends in New York, where he finally began work on *The Little Prince*. The story is narrated by a pilot who has crashed his plane into the Sahara Desert. He meets a little prince visiting from a faraway asteroid. Along the way, the prince also meets Fox and Snake. By late 1942, after spending the spring and summer writing and illustrating, Saint-Exupéry had completed his novel, and in April 1943 it was published in his native language of French *(Le Petit Prince)* and in English.

Saint-Exupéry was eager to return to the war. He decided to join the Free French Forces in Algeria, who were continuing the fight against the Axis powers. Because of his age, at first he had a hard time convincing them to let him fly. He was authorized to fly five dangerous missions. In fact, he flew eight. On July 31, 1944, Saint-Exupéry went on a scouting flight to prepare for military landings in the south of France. His plane disappeared over the water, and he was never seen again.

Over the decades since *The Little Prince* was published, it has gone on to become one of the best-selling novels of all time. In 2003, a small moon in our solar system's asteroid belt was named Petit-Prince in honor of the masterpiece Saint-Exupéry created.

THE LITTLE PRINCE IN THE TWENTY-FIRST CENTURY

The Little Prince is a landmark of literature and one of the most translated and beloved books in the world. It tackles universal topics with a unique philosophical and poetic sensibility. Sixty-five years after the first edition, the Saint-Exupéry Estate decided to bring the character back for a whole new generation . . . and for everyone who has ever loved the boy who sees the world with his heart.

The Little Prince now returns in a series of new adventures that remain true to the spirit of the original work. He will travel from planet to planet chasing the wicked Snake, who wants to plunge the whole universe into darkness. On each planet, the Snake sends bad thoughts into the minds of its inhabitants, making them sad and grim, draining the life out of their planet. The Little Prince must leave his beautiful Rose behind and must use his vision and courage to defeat the Snake, bringing along his friend Fox to save planets in danger across the universe.

ABOUT THE ADAPTERS

After several years in video games and Japanese animation, adapter Guillaume Dorison became literary editor for the publisher Les Humanoïdes Associés in 2006, where he launched the Shogun Collection dedicated to original manga. In June 2010, he founded Élyum Studio with Didier Poli, Jean-Baptiste Hostache, and Xavier Dorison to provide services for the creation of graphic novels. In addition to his position as director of writing for Élyum Studio, he has more than two dozen comics and manga to his credit under the pseudonym IZU, has written several titles in the Explora series on world explorers for French publisher Glénat, and won the 2010 Animeland Prize for best French manga.

Didier Poli, artistic director for the new graphic novel adaptations based on The Little Prince, was born in Lyon in 1971. After graduate studies in applied arts, he worked for various animation studios including Disney. He was working as artistic director for the video game company Kalisto Entertainment when he met Manuel Bichebois in 2001 and began drawing Bichebois' graphic novel series L'Enfant de l'orage. At the 2004 Nîmes Festival, Didier Poli received the Bronze Boar prize for young talent. He continues, along with his work on graphic novels, to work regularly in cartoons and video games as a designer and storyboard artist.